HEADCASE ORIGINS: GROWING UP

KEN MACGREGOR
&
KERRY LIPP

Lycan Valley Press Publications
1625 E 72nd St STE 700 PMB 132
Tacoma, Washington 98404 United States of
America

Printed in the United States of America

Special Edition Bonus Material, February 2022

ISBN-978-1-64562-971-9

HEADCASE Origins: Growing Up stories originally appeared in the 4-part novel serialization. In this supplemental bonus material volume, all four Growing Up stories come together in one place, along with special birthday pieces for Johnny, Katya, Lydia and Gavin.

Additionally, Ken & Kerry created short birthday specials for each character, not included elsewhere.

Enjoy!

BONUS MATERIAL

GROWING UP

Growing Up: Johnny's Story

JOHNNY was at his best on the mound. Out there alone, cap shading his eyes, he stood like a king, or a god maybe.

He eyed the batter: Kevin Donal. A lefty. Kid could hit, too. Last season, he put three over the right field fence.

Kevin Donal also put the moves on Johnny's girl. Sure, all they had done was made out a few times, but they were going steady, dammit! And, nobody, especially not no left-handed slugger *chump* was going to get the better of Johnny Armstrong.

He screwed the ball into the leather of his glove, warming it up. He whispered to it, telling it what he wanted to do, like that Tigers pitcher, Fidrych. The Bird, they called him. Said he was crazy. Said he pulled down his pants on the mound, because he forgot his jock. Crazy or not, the man could pitch.

Now, living in Queen City, Johnny was a Sharks fan, like every other kid in town. But, when they played Detroit, well, it was awful hard to root against the best pitcher in the league. Best in the game.

When he finished talking to the ball, Johnny threw it. A picture-perfect inside fastball, and Kevin Donal went for it.

At the last possible second, the ball dipped, sliding under the bat, and *smack!* into the catcher's glove.

One ball and two strikes later, and the Donal kid walked away with nothing but a bruised ego. Which was just what was gonna happen with Sheila.

Johnny let a couple guys get on base that game, but none of them scored. And, every single time Kevin Donal came up to the plate, Johnny struck him out, always throwing hard, always throwing inside.

The last time, in the eighth inning, Johnny launched a fastball up and in and Kevin took a hack at it but it was impossible to tell if he thought he could hit it or it was just self-defense.

Kevin spat, screamed, and stormed the mound, dragging his Louisville Slugger in the dirt behind him, leaving a trail like a lizard's tail.

Johnny took off his glove and dropped it next to him. He wiped his hands on his white uniform pants and waited. Being on the mound made him seem even taller than he was, and he was already big for thirteen.

Donal came right up, snarling, and poked him in the chest with the business end of the bat. "You're doing it on purpose. Up here throwing junk. Sending me pitches I can't hit. Admit it."

Johnny shrugged. "Shit, man, I didn't tell you to swing at any of those. And what if I am? That is the object of baseball."

"It's cheating. That's what." He poked Johnny a little harder with the bat.

"You're gonna wanna stop that now."

Donal sneered. "Stop what? This." He poked Johnny again.

Johnny snatched the bat from him with one hand. Splinters flew as he broke the hardwood over his knee masking the pain with a vicious smile. Pointing the jagged end at Donal, he said, "Back off. You lost fair and square. Suck it up, buttercup. Now get off my mound."

Donal smacked the half-bat aside and swung a left hook at Johnny's face.

Johnny took it, rolled with it, minimizing the damage. He dropped the bat pieces and laid into the kid. Both fists hitting over and over: body blows, clips to the face.

Donal put his hands up, but Johnny was too fast. His hands found the holes in the other boy's defenses and his fists hammered home.

The Little League coach ran up to the mound yelling his head off, but Johnny only heard noise; he couldn't make out words.

Donal looked at the coach, dropping his guard for a half-second.

Johnny tagged him full-force, rattling Donal's teeth and putting his lights out.

"Damn it, Armstrong! What are you thinking? This is *baseball*, not the boxing ring. You're out!"

"What the hell, Coach? He came at me and I defended myself and you're gonna bench me now?"

"Don't talk back to me, boy. You're out. You're off the team. You're out of Little League. You'll never play in this town again."

Johnny stared at the man. Up on the mound, he was the same height. "You're kicking me out of baseball?"

"Yeah. You're a damn hooligan, Johnny."

"He came at me, and I defended myself. What am I missing here?"

"Look at him! He doesn't have a nose anymore."

Johnny shrugged and held his ground.

"What you gonna do, hit me too?" The coach sneered. "I don't go down as easy as a kid, Johnny."

Johnny hit him on the cheekbone with a left, then dropped into a crouch, ducking the man's clumsy swing. He came up hard with an uppercut. His whole body was behind it.

The coach fell on his butt, stunned.

"Baseball's my life," Johnny told him.

The coach spat out a tooth around his unhinged jaw. "Not anymore."

Johnny turned in a slow circle, looking at each of his teammates, coaches, opponents and fans in the crowd. Every one of them avoided his eyes as they inspected the grass, whispered to each other or pretended to stare at the horizon.

Johnny walked to the dugout and grabbed his bag and headed home without another word.

It wasn't until he reached his front door that the pain kicked in. He looked down at his hands. His knuckles were busted open and though the blood had dried, it left some nasty smears on his white baseball pants. Some drips landed all the way down on his cleats. He could barely move his fingers or his wrists. Nothing felt broken, but he didn't doubt severe sprains and then some in both hands. But none of that hurt as much as getting booted from the team by that smug coach, who'd never had his back.

He'd been pitching a solid game! So what if he threw a lot of pitches high and inside? He never hit a person, never even got warned by an umpire. And now that fucking Donal took something else from him. While his coach, of all people, sided with Donal.

Unbelievable.

Thinking about all this brought the rage back all over again and he forgot about the pain. All Johnny wanted to do was break shit or hurt someone. He tried breathing deep, tried counting to ten, tried pacing through the kitchen, but he couldn't bring himself to see anything but red.

With the words of his coach echoing in his head, Johnny forgot all about the pain in his wrists and fists. He went to the basement and took it all out on the heavy bag. Sweat poured down his face, his lungs burned, and his fists throbbed, but he kept going until he nearly collapsed from exhaustion and a desperate need for water.

Johnny left the bag swinging and turned to head up the stairs, but let out a gasp when he saw his father sitting on them, waiting, with a bottle of water in one hand and two bags of frozen peas on the step beside him.

"Let me see," his father said.

Johnny chewed his lip a moment before he held out both his bloody, swollen hands. The bruises had settled in looking like black and blue camouflage. His father shook his head.

"Jesus Christ. Kid, the only thing bigger than your temper might be your tolerance for pain."

Johnny looked down, didn't meet his father's eyes.

"Maybe my hatred for injustice," Johnny muttered.

"We'll talk about it. Do we need to go to the hospital?"

Johnny shook his head.

"Okay, go ice your hands while I make us some dinner."

Johnny realized how hungry he was when he smelled the ground beef sizzling in the skillet. He'd tried to help his father cook, but his father refused, which Johnny secretly appreciated because he didn't know if he'd even be able to feed himself. His hands felt ruined.

"Your coach called me at work."

"I'm surprised he could talk."

His father smacked his fist on the table. Johnny jolted.

"This is not funny, kid. It was your other coach. The one you clocked is going to be on an all-milkshake diet for at least six months. I'm trying to finish up my day at work, feeling bad enough already that I'm missing your game and then guess what? Out of nowhere, I get a flustered call from a coach saying that you beat up a player on the other team, broke a bat over your knee and punched out your own coach. What in the blue hell happened out there?"

Johnny sighed.

"I was pitching, throwing a pretty good game, and Kevin Donal comes up for the fourth time. I'd struck him out three times already and I got him to take a wild swing at a high inside fastball."

His father held up a hand to silence him.

"How high and inside?"

"C'mon, Dad, if I wanted to hit him in the head, we both know that's what I would've done. I was just looking to humble him. Anyway, he swung and missed and charged the mound with his bat. Poked it into my chest and started with the threats, so I snatched the bat from him, and broke it over my knee. I thought that'd be enough, but I was wrong. He threw a punch, so I took it, and then I beat the shit out of him. Coach comes over to break it up, tells me I'm out of control and not only benches me, but kicks me off the team right there on the mound. He called me a hooligan, and I guess I proved him right."

"Jesus, kid," his father said and patted him on the shoulder. "I'm not mad; I can't be. Not at you defending yourself and standing your ground. But it's bad, Johnny, real bad. They're talking about suspending or expelling you from school, maybe even pressing charges."

"I didn't do anything wrong."

"Maybe you didn't, kid, but that doesn't really matter, does it? It's your word against theirs and those coaches carry a lot more credibility than a loose cannon thirteen-year-old your size. The world is full of injustice, and this is the kind of shit you can step in if you don't control that temper."

"You can't be blaming me for this, you just can't," Johnny fumed.

"I'm not, Johnny. But you've got to be aware that, in the real world, doing the right thing, standing up for yourself, or even defending yourself can have dire, life-altering consequences. You've got to pick your spots and realize that the hill you're defending may not always be worth dying on, even if it isn't your fault."

Johnny opened his mouth.

"No," his father said. "No more. Don't argue with me. Just think about it. Think about no more baseball, possibly no more school, and the pain that's flaring through both your hands. This isn't a punishment, but a lesson about actions and consequences. I need you to think hard and soak it all in, and if we need to talk more tomorrow or whenever, we will. For now, eat."

Johnny struggled to feed himself, but declined help when his father offered. After dinner his father gave him a half-dozen ibuprofen. Johnny swallowed them.

"Now head on upstairs and take a nice long shower, ice those wrists again afterward and get a good night's sleep. Tomorrow might really suck."

Johnny nodded.

"Thanks, Dad."

His father smiled, and hugged him.

Johnny walked to the bathroom on leaden feet.

After a couple weeks, Johnny's hands and wrists were pretty much healed. He'd kept them wrapped for the first couple days, but after that was able to use them, though stiff and clumsy.

He tried not to dwell on the fact that he couldn't play ball, but of course he did. He wrote a letter to the coach, apologizing for hitting him. He got one in return that said the coach appreciated the apology, but that it changed nothing.

What did that leave him? His grades were okay. He wasn't dumb, and usually wasn't lazy. He just didn't care that much about the War of 1812, or how to conjugate verbs in French. All he wanted to do was pitch for the Majors.

To make matters worse, when Sheila heard about what happened on the pitcher's mound, she refused to speak to Johnny.

No baseball.

No girlfriend.

"No point," he said aloud.

"What's that?"

"Nothing, Dad. Just grumbling about the whole thing, you know?"

His father gave him a long, considering look. "Yeah. I get that."

Johnny studied his dad: the scar tissue around his eyes, the broken nose, and the big, swollen knuckles. He had been a heavyweight contender, but never quite good enough to make a run for the title fights.

"What?"

Johnny shrugged. "Maybe I could box."

His dad put his coffee cup down. "It's a hard life, kid."

"I know."

"I'm not gonna tell you 'no.' I mean, you've got a solid foundation already."

"Thanks to you."

His dad smiled. "Well, yeah. Had to teach my kid how to defend himself. What kind of father would I be otherwise?"

"So?"

"All right. We'll go to the gym Saturday. I'll set you up with Vinny. He'll give you the basics. If you have an aptitude for it, we'll find someone to push you beyond that."

Since Johnny had already learned the basics from his own dad, Vinny covered the rest. He focused on footwork and defense, since those were Johnny's weaknesses. In a few months, Vinny called Johnny's dad over. "Kid's a natural. Picks it up fast. He's ready to spar with a welterweight, I think."

"Hold off on that for a while, Vin. I'm not even sure I want him to box, you know? Sport hasn't really done me any favors."

"You were good, man."

"Not good enough."

"Whatever. Not gonna argue with you. If not this, then what's the kid gonna do?"

"I was thinking bail bonds. Like you."

Vinny watched Johnny lay into the speed bag. His fists were almost a blur. At only thirteen, this kid was already looking formidable. "It can get dangerous."

"Yeah."

"Pays good though."

"Yeah."

"It were my kid? I'd say no. But, it ain't my kid."

"Yeah."

"You want me to show him the ropes, I'll do it."

"Do it."

"So, how's this work?"

Vinny looked at him. "Pretty simple, really. We get the bad guys, and bring 'em back to jail."

"Sounds easy enough."

Vinny smiled. "Can be. Sometimes, though, they don't wanna go."

"Makes sense, I guess."

"Right. Sure. But, that's when it gets complicated. No gloves out here, chief. This is the real world."

"Okay. So, you got any 'real-world' advice on gettin' the bad guys?"

Vinny nodded thoughtfully. "You hit the soft parts of their bodies with the hard parts of yours. And, you hit the hard parts of their bodies with something else."

"Vinny?"

"Yeah, kid?"

"That's the best advice I've ever heard."

"Thanks."

Their 'client,' a cowboy with a metal briefcase, stepped out of the motel room door.

Vinny nudged Johnny and they crossed the lot toward him.

He almost had the key in the door when Johnny called out. "Marty!"

The cowboy turned, looking puzzled. "I know you, kid?"

Johnny shook his head. "Not yet. I'm a big fan though."

"What?"

Johnny kicked him in the nuts, hard.

With a whoosh of air, the cowboy collapsed forward, losing his grip on the briefcase.

Johnny grabbed it off the pavement, and hit the cowboy in the head three times.

The guy was out. Blood trickled from his nose and dribbled toward the storm drain.

Vinny slow-clapped. "Yup. That's the way to do it."

"Hey, just following the hard part/soft part advice. Told you it was good. Went a lot better than my last fight, which was all fist against skull."

"Sometimes that's unavoidable," Vinny said squatting down. "Help me roll this fat ass over."

Johnny helped Vinny flip the cowboy

onto his belly and cuffed his hands behind his back.

"You only made one mistake," Vinny said, "but it's a big one."

Johnny's eyes flicked from the cowboy to Vinny where they lingered, looking for some kind of hint.

"Got me stumped," Johnny said.

"Unless it's life and death, don't ever knock out anyone over three hundred pounds. This is gonna suck," Vinny said kicking Marty in the ass.

"Can't we just... you know, use that smelly stuff they use to wake people up on TV? Don't you have that?"

Vinny laughed and shook his head.

"The way you're built and the way you move and fight Johnny, sometimes it's hard to remember you're barely a teenager. He didn't lose consciousness at the sight of blood, you scrambled his brains with that briefcase. Hell, he might be in a coma."

Johnny made a face.

"Don't sweat it, kid. You don't do that and he gets a chance to pull a weapon on you, it could end a whole lot worse."

To prove his point, Vinny frisked the body, removing two guns and a knife. A shoulder holster, ankle holster and belt sheath.

Johnny's stomach twisted when he saw the weapons and realized how easily things could've gone sideways.

"So, you just turned me loose on this guy armed to the teeth?" Johnny said, his face reddening, temper threatening to flare.

Vinny shrugged.

"I was pretty sure you'd be fine, and I was right."

Johnny's lips curled into an angry sneer and his fists balled up.

"Jesus, kid, your dad wasn't kidding. Look, don't get mad at me because I trained you well and sort of had full confidence in you. And if it went off the rails, I had your back, even if it didn't look like it. Trust me. Okay?"

Johnny said nothing. Didn't blink.

"I'm gonna get the car, so we don't have to carry this fat fuck across the parking lot.

While I'm gone, take a breath and cool off. We won. Everything's fine."

Vinny turned his back and took a step toward the car.

Johnny's fists clenched, but instead of pouncing, he heeded Vinny's advice again. Johnny closed his eyes, took a few breaths and composed himself. Not long ago his father had given him some solid advice about choice and consequence. Vinny'd done the same before taking down the cowboy.

The car pulled up and the window rolled down.

"We good?"

Johnny nodded.

"Okay then, open the back door."

Johnny obliged and even with their combined strength, getting the overweight, deadweight cowboy into the backseat was the hardest part of the day. Vinny was right again.

Johnny walked over and picked up the briefcase, which now looked like a flattened Coke can.

"Good god, kid, you sure did a number on his head with that case. Hope they don't need anything in there for evidence, I don't think Houdini could get that open."

"Like you said, use something else for the hard parts."

"Just gotta make sure the bulk of the damage stays on the weapon. If his head looked like this thing, we'd have some explaining to do. Remember, we're bail bondsman, not hitmen. It sort of works the opposite way."

"Noted," Johnny said, walking around to the passenger side.

"You're really something, kid," Vinny said.

He looked at Johnny, looked at the cowboy, looked at the battered briefcase, and smirked.

"A real fucking headcase. I can't wait to tell your dad."

Growing Up:

Katya's Story

"Oh *please*, Mother," Katya's voice sopped with sarcasm. "It's a slumber party. We've had, like, forty of them. There won't be any boys."

"Uh huh. I know, Little Cat. But, I'm your mother; it's my job to worry."

Katya hugged her tight. "You have nothing to worry about. I'll be good. Even if they have good wine, I'll only have one glass."

Her mother shook her head. "Oh no you don't. If they have good wine, you should have two."

Katya grinned. "Mother!"

"Have fun, Little Cat. I'll see you in the morning. We'll finish up your science fair project, get ready to take home another first place trophy. Call if you need a ride."

"Okay."

Katya swept her small duffle onto her shoulder. She kissed her mother on the cheek, flashed her a ten-megaton smile, and exploded out the door.

She wasn't the last one to show up at Bethany's house, but it was a near thing. Bethany welcomed her with a quick hug. She got nods from Veronica, Hannah and Fiona, who pretty much did everything as a unit. The only exception being that Veronica broke her wrist. She still had another week before the cast would come off. It was nearly black with signatures.

Gretchen got up, skipped across the thick gray carpet, and kissed Katya on both cheeks, like the French supposedly do. "Hello, dahling," she drawled, very posh.

"How *do* you do?" Katya replied, in her best high-society manner, executing a curtsey with her pretend gown.

They giggled at themselves and joined the others, just as Brigitte threw open the door with the theatrical relish she was well-known for. "I'm here. The party can finally start."

After homemade mac 'n' cheese, the seven girls climbed the stairs to Bethany's room. Bethany reached behind her chest-of-drawers, and produced a wine bottle.

Brigitte gasped with mock shock. "We're going to get *so* hammered!"

Bethany shook her head. "It's empty."

Brigitte pouted. "Tease."

"Okay," Gretchen said slowly. "Then what's it for?"

Bethany gave her a smile crawling with mischief. "We're going to play spin-the-bottle."

Hannah looked around. "There aren't any boys here, Bethany."

Bethany shrugged. "I don't mind."

Katya said, "I don't either."

Hannah actually scooted back. "Kissing girls is not okay."

"How do you know? Have you ever tried

it?"

"Ew, Bethany. No. Just...gross."

"I kissed my grandma on the lips once. My mom made me," Gretchen said while she mimed gagging and ultimately vomiting.

Everyone laughed, easing some of the tense energy in the room but the tension restored and grew when the laughter went on too long and ratcheted up during the long awkward silence that followed.

"Oh you're all being ridiculous, it's just a peck on the lips not full on tonsil-hockey," Katya said. She snatched the empty bottle from Bethany, then looked at Hannah and added with a wink, "Unless you want it to be."

"You're so weird," Hannah said.

"She's definitely weird," Fiona said.

"And think about how boring our lives would be without a little weird excitement," Veronica said waving her broken arm.

"Hey, participating in the Cooper's Hill Cheese Wheel Race is one kind of excitement, kissing girls is a whole different experience," Hannah said.

"I still can't believe your parents let you do that," Bethany said.

"Yeah, in one you risk serious bodily harm, in the other you just have some fun with your girlfriends," Katya cut in. "How about this for Hannah and anyone else, if you want to be a stick in the mud and don't want to play, then don't. But, if it lands on you, you have the option to truthfully answer a question instead, but you have to answer it."

Hannah bit her lip, considered, and slowly nodded. Everyone else also agreed.

Girls whispered and giggled as Katya placed the bottle on the carpet and directed everyone to sit in a circle around it. While they were still taking their places, Katya gave the bottle a healthy spin and all the girls watched it go around and around before slowing, slowing, about half of them inhaled sharply and held their breath... slowing. And stopped on Hannah.

"Oh come on!" Hannah shouted, immediately getting shushed by all the other girls.

"Just close your eyes, it'll be over in a second and you might even like it," Bethany said.

Katya stood before Hannah with open arms and a beaming smile.

"Nope. No way. Not happening." Hannah shook her head and sat down.

Katya's wide smile turned upside down.

"Fine," Bethany said, "Ask her a question, Kat; she has to answer."

Katya paced for a moment. "Hmmmm. Hannah. What if you were dying, and the only way you could be saved is if a woman or a girl needed to give you mouth to mouth resuscitation. Would this be an issue then? Would you die to keep a woman's lips off your own?"

"Jesus, Katya, have some mercy," Brigitte giggled.

"That's not the same," Hannah shot back, face tomato-red.

"You never know," Katya said. "Maybe you're already not breathing and don't even know it."

"Answer the question, Hannah," Gretchen said.

Hannah glared at her, then at Katya. "Fine. If it was life-or-death, I would do it. Otherwise, no way."

"Who's up next?" Bethany asked.

Veronica raised her good hand. "Me!" She gave the bottle a mighty spin; it slowed to a stop, and the neck was pointing to Katya.

"My lucky day, I guess," Katya said. She crawled on hands and knees across the circle of girls and grinned at Veronica.

Veronica was smiling, but now it faltered. "You guys? We're not going to talk about this at school, right?"

"Nope," Gretchen said. "What happens at Bethany's, stays at Bethany's."

"Okay." She looked Katya in the eye. Her smile was back. "Bring it, *chica*."

Katya put her hands gently on the sides of Veronica's head. She brought her lips up to meet the other girl's. The kiss was soft, and Katya found it nice. A low thrum began to build somewhere behind her navel. A tightening of her abdomen, but not unpleasant. She opened her mouth, just a little, and felt Veronica reciprocate.

The girls touched tongues, and the buzz inside Katya grew stronger. She slid her tongue into Veronica's mouth and kissed her deeply.

Vaguely, she heard gasps and shocked mumblings, but those didn't matter. She was fascinated by the feelings waking up inside her.

Veronica draped her arms over Katya's shoulders, pulling her closer. The rough plaster of the cast scraped the skin a bit. The kiss went on and on.

From her guts, Katya could feel the vibration moving upward. Her spine straightened as pleasurable heat rose through her torso. It pulsed against the back of her throat, and she sighed as it rolled across her tongue, onto Veronica's.

The other girl jolted back. She put her hand to her mouth. Her eyes were huge. "What did you do?"

Katya shrugged. "I don't know. I felt it,

too. It was nice."

"It was *amazing*, but what was it?"

Bethany tapped Veronica on the shoulder. "What? Tell me what's going on. What happened?"

"My arm doesn't hurt. At all. My arm always hurts, and it feels fine now."

"Oh my god," Brigitte said. "Kat's a witch."

Katya looked at the crowd, her eyes bugging, many words forming in her mind but dying on her tongue. Her confused lips quivered at both the intense kiss she'd just experienced and the odd effect on Veronica's arm. It had to be a coincidence, Katya thought. Veronica was just so elated that she forgot about the pain for a moment or something.

In a flash, Brigitte gripped the wine bottle and raised her hand.

"What did you do to my friend?" Brigitte demanded.

Katya lips moved but no sounds came out.

"Get her," Hannah seethed, red-faced

and still shaking off the embarrassment from the first spin of the game.

"Everyone stop!" Bethany screeched, loud enough to draw the attention of her parents.

They all froze, waiting for parental footfalls or an authoritarian knock on the door. A bunch of girls terrified not only of getting caught playing spin the bottle, but only doing it with other girls. Who knew if that made things better or worse? Thankfully, no one came, but the room collectively held its breath for several moments and the girls calmed down. Then Brigitte set the bottle down in the middle of the group and they all relaxed.

"I'm... I'm sorry. I don't know what came over me," Brigitte said.

Hannah sat and sulked and said nothing.

"It's okay, I'm kind of scared too," Katya said, finally finding her voice. "I... I don't know what just happened, but I promise you, if I am some kind of 'witch' I'd never hurt any of you. You're my friends. You have to believe me."

"I believe you," Veronica said. "I don't know what you did, but it doesn't hurt anymore and I can move all my fingers better now, see?" She danced her fingers around with ease. "And this, watch this," she said.

Veronica stood, raised her casted arm high above her head and let it drop, deadweight, onto Bethany's cherrywood dresser.

The other girls all recoiled but Veronica laughed.

"My idiot little brother hit my cast with a football just this afternoon and the pain damn near brought me to my knees," Veronica said, "I don't know what you did, Katya, but thanks, I think."

Katya got up and gave her a hug, and then they both sat.

"Well, that's all certainly been... interesting," Hannah said, recovering from shock and shame. "So what are we going to do now?"

"I have an idea," Bethany said. She

jumped up, rummaged around in her closet, and came back with a shoebox.

The other girls watched, intrigued by the mysterious box.

Bethany lifted the lid and pulled out something small, and silver, and sleek. She thumbed open the blade of the folding knife and said, "Let's see what else you can do."

Katya looked at the knife like it was a dead rat.

"I don't think..." she started.

"It'll be fine," Bethany said. "Just think of it as an experiment, or a test." She picked up the knife and Katya felt her stomach come alive with anxiety. "I just got this. It's pretty sharp, I think." Bethany set the blade against her left forearm. "Here goes nothing."

She cut. For a moment, it was just a line on her skin. Then, it opened, the sides separating to reveal fat and muscle. The crevice filled with blood and it spilled over.

"Shit," somebody whispered.

"It's too deep. I think I messed up," Bethany said. Her voice was small and shaky.

Brigitte whipped off her T-shirt, wrapping it tight around the wound. "Call 9-1-1. Now."

"No," Katya said. She was calm. "I got this." She moved in, taking Bethany's face in her hands. "I got this." She kissed her friend on the mouth.

After a long time, she came up for air, and Bethany grinned.

"You're a hell of a kisser." She took off the blood-soaked shirt. There was a thin line of scar tissue where she'd cut her arm. It was barely noticeable.

"Thanks," Katya said. "But, please don't do that again."

"Okay."

"Guys?" Brigitte held up a hand like she was in class. "Can I borrow a shirt?"

They all laughed. Bethany got her a clean shirt and soaked the other one in cold water.

Veronica put her hand over Katya's own. "Kat, I don't think you're a witch, but...what are you?"

Katya shook her head. "I have no idea,

but it can't be bad, right? If I can heal people, I mean?"

They mumbled their agreement.

"It's not natural though," Brigitte said. Bethany glared at her. Brigitte shrugged. "Just saying."

"Feels natural," Katya said. "Feels right. Guys? Please don't tell anyone, okay? Not until I figure this out? I don't want people to think I'm a freak."

"Even if you are," Brigitte said.

"Even if I am."

"Okay," Brigitte said.

The others promised.

"Thank god. Now, can we please watch a movie, or something normal?"

Growing Up: Lydia's Story

Lydia glanced back at Webster Groves High School. At any moment, the bell would ring, the doors would bang open and hundreds of kids would pour out. Right now though, it was quiet.

She turned on the speed. Her pink pigtails rose on the wind like streamers on the handlebars of a bicycle as she sprinted. The St. Louis suburb blurred around her as, with grace, she dodged every trash can and pothole in her path. The air felt fresh on her face and before the buses back at school were even loaded with students, she slowed to a walk and strolled up her driveway, eager to see her mother and receive her birthday present.

Lydia's smile faded and her face fell when she walked in the front door. She could already smell the booze. Sadness and anger fueled her tears. Her mother sprawled in a recliner with her head hanging at an angle that looked painful. An empty bottle of vodka sat wedged between her legs.

"No, Mom. Not *today*. You promised," Lydia yelled as she slammed the front door, splitting the frame. The whole house shook. *That was weird,* she thought, but was too pissed off to care.

She strode over and plucked the bottle from her mother's lap. Only an ounce or so remained, sloshing against the sides. Lydia gripped the woman's shoulder and shook her.

"Wake up! It's my birthday, remember? You promised, Mom."

Her mother didn't move or make a sound. Anger flared up from the bottom of Lydia's feet all the way to her ears. She pulled a hand back and slapped her mother right across the face. It sounded like a steak tossed off a balcony hitting concrete. Bone cracked. Lydia left a blood-red handprint on her mother's cheek, which now hung grotesquely unhinged.

Lydia stared at her own hand. She'd only meant to rouse her mother, not break her jaw. She flexed her fingers and felt a power coursing through her. After losing herself in the moment, shocked at her own strength and her capacity for violence, she noticed that despite it all, her mother hadn't even flinched.

She checked her mother's breathing and pulse and found nothing.

Did I just kill her?

No.

Her mother's skin was cool to the touch. After the impact of everything settled, Lydia noticed the empty bottle of pills sitting on the end table.

She screamed. All rage and no sorrow.

"You fucking promised you'd tell me today. You owe me!" She yelled into her mother's face and struck her again and again until she collapsed into a crying ball of hate and guilt.

But her mother never woke up.

Exhausted and demoralized, Lydia fell asleep at the foot of the recliner.

She woke hours later. Sunlight through the windows had faded to darkness and only a lamp lit the room. She looked at the recliner, at her dead and disfigured mother, and it all came back. Despite the abuse to her face, her mother's mouth was stretched into a wide grin. Lydia wrinkled her nose and stuck out her tongue.

"Rigor mortis. Gross."

She stood, stretched, and looked at the prescription bottle on the end table. Under it sat an envelope with her name written on it. With shaking hands she tore the envelope open. A small piece of metal fell out and clinked onto the glass of the table. Lydia glanced down at an ornate key.

After another look at her mother's dead

face, Lydia unfolded the papers inside.

Lydia,

I can't imagine how you're feeling right now, but I promised you, and this note will show you that I kept my promise. I wish I could've done this in person, but I just can't. You don't know what it's been like, looking after you for the last thirteen years. You're such a good, special girl, and none of this is your fault. Mine neither. It's all beyond our control, but maybe after you read this, you'll have the strength to take that control back. Or maybe not. The choice will be yours and yours alone, and even if I can somehow see you from the afterlife, I'll never judge you for your decisions.

You're special, Lydia. I know you've known that you aren't like the other kids for a long time. From the natural color of your hair to the speed you can turn on that leaves everyone in the dust. Now that you're a teenager you'll experience a lot more changes, changes that I can't bear to witness. One of these days, soon, your wings will show themselves, but I think you'll be able to hide them if you choose.

Lydia almost dropped the letter. *Wings?* She blinked and read on.

And though you're at the beginning age of puberty you will develop to sexual maturity in a matter of days, maybe even faster, whenever those days begin. If the research I've done on your kind is accurate, it's likely to start today.

You're a succubus, baby. Half-human, half-demon. But that doesn't mean you're doomed to do horrible things! I've lied to you about your father all along. He's an incubus, pure evil. A bad, bad man. He couldn't seduce me, so he beat me and raped me. I ended up with you, and, as a final parting gift, he cursed me. Baby, I promise it's his fault, not yours, but he cast a spell on me, and every time I lay eyes on you, or hear your voice, it takes me right back to that night. The brutal beating and the violent rape. I relive it day after day. I experience the physical pain and emotional torture. I promised myself I'd see you through to your teenage years, and once they arrived I'd come clean. I always knew I'd kill myself too, but I kept that part from you, obviously.

Lydia, you're a smart, tough and beautiful girl. You are capable of living your own life without my guidance. More than capable. You can make your own decisions and live life as you please, but I hope you do your best to do right, even in this messed up world we live in. In the end, maybe you can even balance out some of the atrocities your father has inflicted on this world.

I leave you with a key and a decision. The key goes to the box sitting on your pillow. Call it a birthday present. Your decision lies in that box.

I love you baby, and I'm sorry. None of this is your fault.

You'll be okay, I promise.

Happy birthday.

All my love,

Mom

Lydia read the note three times, wiping tears from her eyes with the back of her hand. She looked at her mother, and loved and hated her at the same time. The suicide felt like betrayal and it burned like fire, but it was softened by what her mother had endured to bring her to this point. Lydia stroked her mother's cheek with trembling lips, and swallowed hard. She shook her head, picked the key up off the end table, and headed upstairs.

Her footsteps on the stairs were the only sound. She shook with something close to terror. An inexplicable and illogical sensation that she wasn't alone, that something — a monster or worse — waited for her at the top of the stairs. She'd never been afraid of such things, but with her mother's corpse downstairs and the horrible story of her history ringing in Lydia's ears, the dangers of the world began to feel very real.

She tiptoed through the upstairs, searching all the rooms and closets before she was satisfied no one else was in the house. Maybe she was just avoiding the final gift from her mother. She felt exhausted and just didn't know anymore. She pushed her bedroom door open.

Her room remained undisturbed except for the beautiful black box resting against her headboard. The smooth wooden box was bigger than she'd imagined it would be. Maybe two feet long and a foot across. She glanced around her room, saw nothing out of place and no one waiting to snatch her. She stepped forward.

Gripping the key between thumb and index finger, she gently pushed it into the keyhole and gave it a delicate twist. The lid was silent as it swung open.

Two items lay inside. A photo and a purse.

The picture was black and white: a man with a charming smile, scheming eyes, and a sharp widow's peak. On the bottom of the photograph, written in red capital letters:

YOUR FATHER.

She flipped the glossy photo over and saw that her mother had provided her with a name and an address. She didn't recognize the name — James Silvercreek — but the address was right here in St. Louis.

Next to the photo was a Coach purse. Lydia smiled. She'd wanted one for a long time. She picked it up by the straps. It was heavy. Unzipping it, she pulled out a few bundles of cash. At least a few thousand dollars.

Holy shit, Mom.

An envelope poked up from one bundle of cash. She opened it and pulled out a voucher for a plane ticket to Alaska.

Alaska? Well, that was about as far from St. Louis as she could get. She could have a new home and a fresh start.

She had a decision to make.

Confront her father?

Kill him?

Or just get the hell out of here?

Lydia believed there were two sides to every story and thought that at the very least, she might be able to learn more about herself from seeing her father. Her mother wouldn't lie about him would she? Before today Lydia never would've thought so, and still didn't, but her birthday had been one massive curveball. Maybe her mother was delusional, unstable. Hard to trust someone who just committed suicide.

After a final glance around her bedroom, Lydia made her way down the stairs. At the base of the stairs she paused to look at her mother. Walking over, she planted a kiss on her cool forehead. "I forgive you and I'm sorry. I love you, Mom. Thank you."

And she walked out the front door.

On the porch, she hesitated, squeezing her new purse against her ribs. She glanced again at the plane ticket, then at the St.

Louis address. She put both back in the purse with the cash and zipped it shut.

She ran at full speed, zooming past a man walking his dog. She caught his surprised expression as his hair flew back in the breeze she made. The dog whined and dipped its head.

A few minutes later, she stood in front of her father's house. It was small, beige, and boring. It looked old too, like it had been built two hundred years ago. Her face flushed with exertion and her lungs heaved for fresh air as sweat spilled down her face. She'd never gone that far that fast. Had to be at least fifteen miles.

She reached up to knock and her gut twisted in knots. The cramping pain was so intense, she fell to the ground, clutching her midsection. Writhing on the porch floor gritting her teeth, she felt like she was being turned inside out. She felt nauseated and scared as red blood blossomed on her jeans from between her legs. She knew what it was, but she was shocked and repulsed anyway. There was so much of it. She wondered if it would ever stop.

The skin on her chest tightened, stretching painfully. Glancing down, she watched as breasts formed almost instantly. She went from nothing to a C-cup in about seven seconds. Her eyes gaped in wonder at her two new features. Tears she couldn't control rolled down her cheeks as she stared at the doorstep. She sniffed once, trying to get herself together.

"What the hell?"

Her head snapped up at the male voice. He stood in the open doorway, hands on his hips, smirking at her. Sky blue curls (*azure*, she thought, recognizing it from art class) covered his head, but it somehow suited him. His eyes were so dark they might have been black. Those eyes narrowed, blue brows forming an angry v-shape.

"Who are you and why are you bleeding on my porch?"

She pushed herself to her knees. The blood cooled on her pants. It was sticky and uncomfortable, but she ignored it. With effort, she stood up. Glancing down once more at the impossible bulges under her shirt, she shook her head, cleared it.

"I'm your daughter, asshole."

For a long time, he stared at her. His gaze traveled from her pink hair down past the blood on her pants to her sneakers. His eyes crawled their way back up, lingering for a couple seconds on her breasts. She shuddered. He studied her face and an eyebrow arched.

"Colleen is your mother?"

"Was. She killed herself this morning."

"Mm. That happens sometimes. You must be about thirteen, then…"

"Lydia. And, yeah. Thirteen. Today is my birthday."

"Happy birthday, Lydia."

She spat. "Go fuck yourself." She could barely believe the words coming out of her mouth, but it felt good to say them. It felt *adult*.

He stepped forward and walked a slow circle around her. He fingered one of her pigtails and she jerked her head away. In front of her once more, he smiled and patted her cheek.

She flinched.

"Don't fucking touch me."

He smiled and shook his head.

"My little girl, all grown up. Well, almost all. No wings yet. But they'll be along soon. So, Lydia, tell me, what brings you here? Why did you seek out your father?"

"I wasn't sure at first, but now I know that I'm going to kill you."

He laughed and nodded.

"Ah. Good. Excellent. Embrace your dark side."

It was her turn to laugh.

"Please. Don't give me that Hollywood bullshit about good and evil. I know I'm good. I was raised to be good. And, if I kill you, I'll be eradicating evil. Which means, I'm still good. God, I can only imagine all the women you've raped."

He flinched, just for a second.

"You think you have it all figured out. I don't expect you to understand. Humans never do and half-breeds are even worse. Very well then, Lydia, my sweet daughter.

It'll be your funeral. So tragic. Dead before you even get your wings."

She grinned at him. Then, as fast as she could, using all her strength, she slugged him. His head snapped back. Blood flowed from his nose and he looked shocked. Then he smiled. The blood stopped flowing. He backhanded her. She flew eight feet off the porch over the steps and slid another three on the grass.

Before she could get up, he was on her, raining blows on her face with his fists. It hurt, but not nearly as much as she expected. He stopped whaling on her and stared. With a single knuckle, he tapped on her collarbone. It sounded like he was hitting hard plastic.

"I'll be damned," he said, smiling at the play on words.

"What?" Her skin felt hard and weird and … wrong. "What did you do to me?"

"Not me. I didn't do this. But, most of us don't get a carapace until adulthood. You'd be formidable someday, if I wasn't about to kill you. Such a shame."

"We'll see about that."

She brought her knee up hard and smashed his groin. Agony flashed on his face and he fell off of her. She stood up and kicked him in the balls again.

"Not my nuts!" he seethed through clenched teeth as his pale face turned green.

"Figures. An Incubus's glass jaw is his balls. Learn something new every day." She shrugged, then laughed. "Time for some serious pain."

She stomped her foot down and *thunk*.

Her father transformed. A layer of dark, segmented armor covered him from head to toe.

"Carapace." His slit of a mouth, insect like, grinned at her.

Lydia frowned and flipped him over onto his back, and hooked her hands in his armpits. He must have weighed two hundred and twenty pounds, but she lifted him with ease. Arching her back and gritting her teeth, she *pushed*. The wings she could feel hiding beneath her skin slid out and unfolded. Big and beautiful like a butterfly.

She fluttered her new wings a few times to get the feel of them. And then…she flew, her father still in her grasp.

About two hundred feet up, he groaned, shook his head, and shouted at her.

"Damn it, Lydia. Put me down this instant."

She laughed. It sounded so … *parental.* She flew a little higher, wrapped her legs around his waist and squeezed a little. She put her face down by his and whispered in his ear.

"Can you fly, Daddy?"

"Fuck you and your mother."

"Wrong answer." She flipped him upside down and dropped him.

It took a while for him to fall. She expected him to sprout wings and fight back. He didn't. When his head hit the ground, she heard the crunch from way up in the sky. When she landed lightly on the grass next to him, she was surprised to find him breathing. Unconscious, broken, bloody, but still alive. The carapace was gone. *Must revert to normal when you pass out. Good to know.*

With the adrenaline rush and triumph of victory, Lydia burst into giggles and wondered if maybe she was losing it. She grasped a handful of her father's shirt and, pausing to snag her Coach purse, she dragged him inside his house.

She hauled him through the kitchen, where she pulled a carving knife from a wooden block. Then she found the bathroom and tossed him in the tub.

Her father moaned. She turned toward him and held up the big knife.

"Incubus. Sex demon." She grinned at him. "So, the source of your power, logically, would be…"

She grimaced and grabbed his penis with her left hand, stretching it. With a quick swipe, she severed it near the base.

His eyes snapped open then and he gurgled wetly, building in volume until it developed into a full on scream. She stabbed him in the throat and he went back to gurgling. She tossed her father's prick in the tub. Methodically, she cut him to pieces.

This is a monster, she thought. *I am doing this*

for the good of the world. No other women will be victimized by this demon. She managed not to puke, but it was a near thing.

Afterward, Lydia stripped off her clothes, got in the tub and pulled the curtain closed. She had to push parts of her father aside with her foot. She turned the shower on full hot and moved the nozzle around to rinse the blood from the walls, the tub, herself and what remained of the demon.

Exiting the shower and catching her reflection in the mirror brought her up short. She touched her face with armored fingers. There was a click on contact and the vaguest sensation of touch. She was smooth, shiny, insectile. It was cool and creepy all at once. She wished it would go away. And at once it did and her skin softened to its normal texture.

There stood naked Lydia with wet pink pigtails, weird new breasts and a thatch of pink hair between her legs. That was new, too, and complemented her budding adult figure.

When she got tired of staring at her new

anatomy, she dried off with one of his towels. Pulling the shower curtain down, she spread it on the floor. Then, she piled the pieces of him on it, along with her clothing, and wrapped it into a bundle. She hefted it over her shoulder and walked confident and naked around his house, trying doors until she found stairs going down to the basement.

The cold concrete floor sucked the heat from the soles of her feet as she fed bloody clothes into the furnace. It was one of the old, huge ones that have been out of date since the 1970s.

Once her clothes were incinerated, she turned her attention to her father's remains. They were moving, shifting. The right forearm nudged against the hand and wrist and fused together.

"Oh no you don't." She tossed the big piece into the flames. She followed it with all the other pieces. She saved his head and prick for last. Holding one in each hand, she frowned. "Decisions, decisions."

Her father's eyes opened. She jumped.

"You can't really kill our kind. I'll come back to this plane. I'll find you and make you pay." His eyes flicked to her other hand. "Is that my dick?"

She gaped at him. "How can you talk without lungs?"

He rolled his eyes. "Seriously? I'm a talking severed head and you want to know where the air is coming from?"

Lydia shrugged. "I'm kind of into science and shit at school."

The head smiled. The eyes crinkled at the corners. "How are your grades?"

She shook her head. "I don't really want to talk about this."

She casually tossed the severed penis into the flames and they both watched it burn.

"Man, you really have a mean streak. I have to say, I'm kinda proud."

"Shut it, you."

She clamped his chin up and heard his teeth click hard together through his closed mouth and then chucked his head into the furnace. She could still hear his voice through the flames.

"Ow. Hot. This isn't over, Lydia. You bitch. Ow. Really hot. Ew. Burning hair. I hate that smell. Ow, ow, ow, ow."

Even after the head stopped talking, she could hear the jaw clacking against the upper teeth and later, even that white noise faded to black.

After her father burned to ash and bone, she went upstairs. She looted his drawers and closet and found a t-shirt long enough to use as a dress. Wrapping one of his neckties around her waist as a belt, she checked the mirror. Her face looked normal. She didn't look like a crazy person, which surprised her.

She felt a hot wave of nausea course through her stomach when the silence of the empty house registered what she'd just done. *He was evil, pure evil,* she told herself and then another thought twisted her stomach.

What if he had a family of his own?

She frantically searched the house, tore open drawers and looked for photos. She found nothing. She was safe, but she promised herself that if this would be her course in life, she'd be more careful.

"I'm betting that's gonna catch up with me later and I'm gonna need years of therapy," she told her reflection. "But, right now, I'm good. I know I did the right thing."

With the smell of burning clothes and a burning body emanating through the house, she walked out the front door with her purse on her shoulder. Her mother and father were gone, and there would certainly be questions about their deaths. She had friends, but no one she considered really close. Nothing anchored her to St. Louis.

Going to Alaska, and fading into obscurity, at least for a while, was unbelievably attractive.

The airport was about twelve miles away. For a moment, she considered sprouting her new wings and flying there, but she didn't want to rip holes in the shirt. Besides, it was a nice day for a walk.

First, though, she would hit The Clover, the high-end women's fashion shop on Big Bend. There was a fat stack of cash in her Coach purse and she'd be damned if she was going to wear a dead demon's t-shirt any longer than necessary.

The gate guard looked at the passport photo and back at Lydia. He did this five times. She sighed.

"You're looking at me like I'm wanted for murder or something. It's not like this is even another country. What's the hold up?"

The man handed her the passport.

"How long ago was that taken?"

"I don't know. Year and a half maybe?"

"Kid, you grew up a lot in a year and a half. Go on. Get out of here. Enjoy your stay in Alaska."

She smiled at him and twirled a pink pigtail.

"Thanks, pal. For a minute, I was afraid I'd have to kill ya. Glad I didn't. Buh-bye now." She winked.

Before he could respond, Lydia whirled away, tossed her bag over a shoulder, and strode out of the airport. Stepping outside, she stopped, stunned. A woman stood near her wearing a t-shirt and shorts. Lydia goggled at her.

"It's warm," Lydia mentioned.

The woman glanced at her phone, tapped the screen. "Yup. Sixty-seven. Not bad for May."

"Man, I thought it was going to be freezing."

"Then why aren't you wearing a coat?" The woman looked her over.

"It's because I'm super-tough."

The woman smiled. "Right. Well, that'll serve you well when everything does get covered in ice in a few months." She put out her hand and Lydia took it. "Name's Paula. Paula Stone."

"Lydia. Surname kind of in limbo right now."

Paula nodded. "That's cool. Well, that's my bus. Nice talking to you."

Lydia said goodbye and looked around at downtown Anchorage. It looked like any other American city. She figured out which way was north by the sun, though it was in a weird place in the sky for this time of day, and started walking.

When she was little, she had seen a documentary where people used a curved blade to cut the meat from seals. Lydia wanted to see how it was done. Wanted to hold the tool in her hands, to slice the meat herself. She wanted to taste seal meat, to live with the Inuit tribes in the frozen wastelands. She remembered thinking Alaska was a weird place for her mother to send her, but setting foot outside the airport, she realized just how well her mother knew her.

Lydia walked the streets of Anchorage, heading ever northward, until civilization dropped away. She marveled at her new body. It took forever to tire and didn't seem to need as much food or water as it used to. She was stronger than she'd ever been and loved it. She felt like a superhero.

"Or supervillain, maybe. I mean, I am part demon after all," she scoffed to no one but herself.

After several days travel, she finally arrived at an Alaskan coastal village. Roughly ninety people lived there, year round. They survived mostly off what they pulled from the sea. The houses all needed new paint or siding or both. The whole place looked weather-worn in the extreme.

Two larger buildings dwarfed the houses which were mostly single-story, small family affairs; one by the water was clearly a fishery by the smell. The other big building was called "Moe's" and a neon "Budweiser" sign flashed in the window.

Lydia made a beeline for the bar.

Four men were eating at a table. Their conversation stopped when she walked in. The bartender pushed himself up, scraping the chair on the floor. The only other patron was a thirty-something man at the bar who had a shot in one hand and a beer in the other. It was two thirty in the afternoon.

"Get you something?"

She looked up at the bartender when he spoke. "Are you Moe?"

He chuckled. "Nope. Moe died back in '94. I'm Carl."

"I'm Lydia. I could use some food. What's good?"

"Fish." Laughing, he shook his head. "It's

pretty much all we got."

"Fish it is, then. Thanks." She nodded and sat a few spots down from the drinker.

Carl nodded and slipped through a saloon door behind the bar. The drinker downed the shot and put the glass down hard. She glanced at him.

"Nice hair," he slurred.

"Thanks." She frowned.

"I'm wondering, does the carpet match the drapes?" One of the guys at the table snorted.

"Don't be an ass, Marty."

Lydia smiled at the guy who spoke up. She turned back to the drinker. "I'm only thirteen."

"You look a lot older."

"Can't help that."

"Thirteen, huh? Well, doesn't bother me if it doesn't bother you."

She blinked at him. A hot tear spilled from one eye. She swiped it away. "Are you fucking serious, guy? I'm *thirteen*. I'm a kid, you asshole. What the hell is wrong with you?"

He stood up. He was bigger than she thought.

"You got a filthy mouth, girl."

"I thought they only served fish; not cockroaches." Lydia stood, facing him. The urge to cry had evaporated.

Laughter from the table.

"You think you're funny, you little cunt?" Marty flushed. He lunged at her, grabbing a handful of her shirt. He cocked his fist back. Lydia stood her ground and smirked at him.

"And *I* have a filthy mouth? Go ahead, tough guy. Give it your best shot."

He slammed his fist forward, stopping inches before hitting her face. She didn't blink.

"That was a warning. You keep a civil tongue, or next time, I'll hit you for real."

She grinned. Very deliberately, she enunciated the next words. "Fuck. You."

"I'm almost sorry about this, but I warned you." Marty shook his head. He cocked his hand back again and this time he hit her in the mouth. A tiny trickle of blood oozed from her lip. She never stopped smiling.

"Okay. My turn."

Grabbing his wrist, she twisted it until he let go of her shirt. With the other hand, she hit his chin with an open palm. He left the ground, flew back four feet and hit the floor unconscious.

The four guys at the table were on their feet, but stayed where they were.

"What happened?" Carl came out of the kitchen, wiping his hands on his apron.

"Nothing. How's that fish coming?" Lydia wiped the blood off her lip.

"Almost done. You okay?"

"Fine." She nodded. "Sorry about your friend."

"Marty? He's a dick. Can I ask you something?"

She nodded.

"What are you doing here?"

"I want to learn how to kill seals and how to cut them up with an ulu." She shrugged.

"Why?" His eyebrows shot up.

"Why not?" Lydia shook her head and laughed.

"Fair enough. While you eat, I'll call my buddy Jim. He's an honest to God Inuit; he's got ulus and rocks them old school. Maybe he'll be able to give you some work. Cool?"

Lydia nodded.

"Very cool. " She handed Carl a hundred dollar bill. "And, when the douchecanoe over there wakes up, tell him his drinks are on me. For the headache he's gonna have. Also, let him know if he ever propositions an underage girl again, I'll feed him his own dick."

Carl looked over at the table. The guys there nodded like it was a sure thing. He met Lydia's level gaze.

"I'll do that. I have a feeling things are going to get a lot more interesting around here," Carl said, and handed her a basket of fish and fries.

"I hope so," she said, and took a bite.

Growing Up: Gavin's Story

The light from the hall penetrated Gavin's lids, pulling him out of the dream. It had been a good dream, too: Sandy Parker in a bikini. He hadn't seen her at the pool in real life, but had imagined it many times.

Sandy scattered into a thousand pieces, like glass dropped from the school roof onto asphalt.

Gavin cracked his lids open. "Time is it?"

"Four," his dad said.

"Oh god. This isn't fun, Dad; this is punishment."

"Come on, kid. Get dressed. Wear layers: it's cold, but it's gonna warm up later."

"Why did I agree to this again?" But, his dad was already walking away. He pulled on long johns, jeans, short, then long sleeved shirts, and a sweater. Two pairs of socks, too.

His dad was waiting by the garage door. He wore a bright orange jacket, and handed a matching, smaller one to his son.

Gavin pulled it on. It smelled new.

His dad drove south, toward the woods. They were quiet for a long time.

"Dad?"

"Mm?"

"What if I can't do it? What if I can't pull the trigger, I mean?"

"Doesn't matter."

"It doesn't?"

"Mm-mm. We may not even see a deer. It's the first day of season. You never know."

Gavin thought for a bit. "Yeah. Okay, but what if we do? What if I have one in my sights, and I chicken out?"

"What if you do?"

"Won't you be disappointed?"

"Nope."

Gavin looked at him. He could make out his profile in the pre-dawn dim, but only barely. "Why not?"

"Gavin. This isn't about killing deer. It isn't about hunting even. It's about spending time together, father and son. It's a bonding thing. I don't give a damn if you kill a deer. If one of us does, we'll eat it, and tan the hides for new boots. If not, we'll still have a good time. Okay?"

Gavin nodded. "Okay."

His dad pulled off onto a dirt road that was barely more than a couple ruts between the trees. The car jolted along for a couple miles and opened up to a dirt parking area. There were two cars there, but nobody around. They pulled to a stop and his dad killed the engine.

He got the rifles out of the trunk, and helped Gavin load his.

"You remember all the steps?"

"Yeah. It was two days ago."

"I know. I gotta ask though. Rifle's a dangerous thing. Don't want any accidents."

"Okay, Dad. But, seriously, I got this. I

remember everything you taught me."

His dad ruffled his hair, like he was eight or something.

He glared at the man in mock indignation and smoothed it back down with his free hand.

His dad laughed. "Okay. Come on. Let's go see if we can find that damn blind. Pretty sure I remember how to get there, but you know how it is."

"Yeah," Gavin said. "You get old; your memory starts to go..."

"Smart ass."

His dad led them through the rough woods as if they were on an actual trail, though Gavin couldn't figure out how he knew where to go. It all looked the same to him.

Finally, they came to a couple pieces of plywood screwed together and covered with long grasses. It looked like it had been rotting there since the Civil War.

"This is the blind?"

"Yeah." His dad grinned at him. "You like it?"

"Oh sure. It's palatial."

"Good word."

"Thanks. It was on a vocab test last year."

"See? Told you school was good for you."

"Yeah. So is apple cider vinegar, but it tastes like butt."

His dad laughed. "All right. No more being funny. We need quiet, or we won't see anything all day."

They settled into the blind. Gavin thought he was too tired to stay awake, but the cold kept him sharp. The sun climbed the sky, but the temperature lagged behind.

Gavin's rifle came equipped with a scope. With it, he could see farther even than his mom's powerful binoculars. She used them for bird-watching, and they were good ones. He laid his eye to the scope, slowly panning across the line of trees.

A squirrel chased another who had an acorn in its mouth.

A rabbit grazed on grass, ears twitchy, alert.

There. Something bigger, in the dark,

past the first few trees.

Gavin pitched his voice as quiet as he could. "Dad. I think I see a deer."

His dad looked at where Gavin's rifle pointed, and lined up his own. He whispered back. "Could be. It's big enough. No rack though. Might be a doe."

They both watched the animal moving through the trees. It was getting closer.

It was not a deer.

Gavin drew in his breath. "Dad," he whispered, awed. "It's a wolf."

"Damn. Probably not gonna see any deer at all with that guy around. Might as well pack it in."

"Wait," Gavin said. He watched the wolf slink along, admiring the supple play of muscles under its thick pelt. "God, it's beautiful."

The wolf jerked. Red blossomed on its neck. They heard the shot half a second later.

Gavin's jaw dropped. He lowered the gun. He looked at his dad. Tears fell down his cheeks.

His dad's eyes were shining, too. "Damn it. God damn it. They're a protected species."

Gavin started to get up, but his dad stopped him.

"Wait."

They lay in the blind.

After a few minutes, an orange, camouflage coat appeared, as another hunter tromped out of the trees toward the wolf. He whistled at his kill. "Gotcha."

Gavin's dad stood up slowly. He kept his rifle pointed down.

The hunter heard him and turned.

Gavin trained his rifle on the other hunter, without thinking about what he was doing.

"Hey," his dad said to the guy.

"Hey."

"You know wolves are endangered, right?"

"You a warden?"

"Nope."

"Fuck you care then?"

"I'm not gonna report you or anything,

but I think it's maybe best if you don't hunt here anymore."

"All right. Whatever. I got my quota. I'll get outta here."

The man moved toward the wolf.

"Leave it."

He stopped. "What? It's my kill. I got the right to take it."

"Leave it."

The man moved his rifle up, like he was gonna point it at Gavin's dad.

Gavin's finger rested on the trigger. *Can I do this? Can I kill a man?*

His dad's rifle was up fast, pointed, rock-steady at the other hunter's chest. His voice was hard, uncompromising. "Leave it."

"You're gonna shoot me?"

"Only if I have to."

The man looked at him for a long time. He glanced down at Gavin, seeming to notice him for the first time.

Two barrels stared back.

"Fine. Jesus. Don't have to make a stink about it. I'm going."

"All right. One more thing."

"What?"

"I'm a cop. I memorized the license plates of the vehicles back there. It's habit. Anything happens to my truck, and I'll find you. You'll do time. For the wolf and destruction of property. You understand?"

"Yeah. Shit. I understand. You coulda opened with that, you know? If I'd known you were a cop, I'd have been respectful."

"Should've been respectful anyway."

The hunter grumbled under his breath, but walked away.

Gavin kept his rifle trained on him until he could no longer see him.

"Why did you lie?"

"I didn't want to come back to four flat tires."

"Dad, you're pretty cool, you know."

"I know." He smiled. "Come on."

"What?"

"Help me." He pulled a sharp knife from a sheath at his belt. "We need to field dress that wolf."

Gavin gaped. "We're taking it?"

"Yeah. Not as good as venison, but it'll do. Fur will make good winter gear, too. Besides, I'm not leaving this beautiful, majestic creature to lie here and rot."

They worked together to gut the wolf.

"Dad?"

"Mm?"

"You'd have made a good cop."

"Thanks. I make a pretty decent librarian, too though, right?"

"Yeah. You make a pretty great librarian. Pretty great dad, too, for the most part."

"'For the most part'?"

"Your jokes, man. Some are so bad."

His dad laughed. "All right. I'll own that one. Speaking of, did I tell you the one about the corn muffin and the raspberry muffin in the oven"

"About forty-seven times."

They carried the dead wolf back toward the car.

"Wanna hear it again?"

Gavin laughed. "Sure, Dad."

BONUS
MATERIAL

HAPPY BIRTHDAY

Johnny Headcase's Birthday

by Ken Macgregor

JOHNNY took deep, calming breaths and shifted into a shooter's stance, not for a moment taking his eyes off the wolf.

It was a huge animal, standing almost five feet at the shoulder. Its eyes caught the moonlight and seemed to glow from within. Its fur bristled with menace.

It was maybe forty feet away, growling, low and hungry.

It sprang.

Johnny drew his pistol from his shoulder holster, lightning fast.

The wolf ran alarmingly quick, closing the distance.

Johnny shot it, putting all fifteen bullets in its head, shoulders and chest.

It dropped, unmoving, at Johnny's feet. Johnny reloaded and pointed the barrel down at the supine lupine. He waited.

Fifteen seconds passed. The wolf's body slowly morphed into that of a naked human man. He opened one eye, grinned, and opened the other. "How was that?" he asked.

"Good," Johnny said. "Thanks."

The naked man sat up. "Sure thing. Happy birthday! What do you want to do next?"

Katya's Birthday

by Kerry Lipp

"The biggest cake I've ever baked!" Nick exclaimed, pushing a cart with a massive layer cake on it. A single candle burned at the top, embedded in pastel frosting. Johnny and Lydia clapped.

"That's enormous! It looks like something a stripper jumps out of," Katya said.

"I know it's your birthday, but you could always share," Johnny said.

"What if it's a male stripper?" Lydia asked and poked him.

"Don't ruin my fantasy."

Nick sighed. "Look, could you just blow the damn candle out, the wax is starting to drip into the frosting and ruin the—"

With a low guttural snarl rising to a full-blown howl, the birthday cake exploded covering everyone with cake and icing. A grinning werewolf darted over and put its paws on Katya's shoulders. It licked her face, smearing cake all over her.

"Jesus, Gavin, way to make an entrance," Johnny said.

"Why would you do this to my birthday cake?" Nick asked. "Not only did you demolish the whole thing, it's got… fur all over it."

Gavin reverted to human form wearing only splatters of pink frosting.

"Why do you always do this? That cake looked delicious," Lydia asked.

"Well, if you must know, I did it for the birthday girl, she's got a new device she wants to try out. Right, m'lady?"

"He's right," Katya said, unzipping a bag and pulling out an object that looked like it belonged on a spaceship. She tapped a couple buttons and placed it on the floor. "Here goes."

At once, every piece of fur embedded in

the cake flew through the air and stuck itself to Katya's new invention.

"It works! Way better than a vacuum."

Nick looked horrified.

"Couldn't you have tested it on… like a couch? Do you have any idea how long it took me to make that cake? And I don't even want to know how he got in there."

"Still pretty good though," Lydia said, taking a bite out of a ball of cake in her fist.

"Thanks Lydia," Nick said.

"Not bad," Gavin said.

"Whatever," Nick said. "Just put some pants on."

LYDIA'S BIRTHDAY

by Ken MacGregor

"WHERE are you taking me?" Lydia tested the handcuffs. They were high quality. She might be able to break them, but not without a lot of noise.

"You'll see." The voice was modulated electronically. Lydia couldn't tell anything about whoever had kidnapped her.

The last thing she remembered was getting absolutely shit-faced at her birthday party. There was karaoke and an open bar, and she'd put a huge dent in that bar's supply. Now her mouth tasted like sawdust, and she was blindfolded and restrained. "Could've kissed me first," she mumbled.

She could feel the helicopter going down.

It was one of those stealth jobs, with rotors you can barely hear. *Military? Who did I piss off?*

They landed. Lydia tensed when a hand touched her blindfold. It was torn off quickly. Katya smiled at her. She held a small device by her throat and spoke in that neutral voice. "Surprise!"

She took it away and used her normal voice. "Happy birthday, Lydia!" She opened the chopper door. Frigid air filled the cabin.

Lydia looked outside. She was back in the Alaskan village where she'd lived for years. Where she acquired her first ulus. Several old friends were outside, grinning at her. She hugged Katya, who slipped her a mint. "Thank you. You're the best."

Gavin's Birthday

by Ken MacGregor

Gavin's head jerked around. He sniffed the air again, just to be certain. *That's blood, all right.* Sliding out of his shoes, he padded silently down the hall toward the apartment. Outside the door, he paused, inhaling deeply.

He could smell his friends in there. And blood. So much blood. If someone had killed his friends…

Growling low, he turned the knob. Unlocked. He came in fast and low, ready to fight, ready to change, to become a wolf if necessary.

The apartment was dark. Shadowy figures lurked across the room. Two of them.

He tensed to spring. Someone was behind him.

The lights came on.

"Surprise!" Three voices. Johnny, Lydia, and Katya.

They were in his place. On the table: a huge pile of raw steak, oozing blood on the platter. A candle was sticking out of the top piece. Katya lit it.

"Happy birthday, dude," Johnny said, clapping him on the back.

"I almost *killed* you guys."

Lydia snorted. "You wish. We could take you."

Katya kissed him on the cheek. "Blow out the candle, tough guy."

Gavin did. Then he ate the meat. All of it.

.

AVAILABLE NOW FROM LVP PUBLICATIONS:

HEADCASE

A NOVEL IN 4 PARTS BY KEN MACGREGOR & KERRY LIPP

WWW.LYCANVALLEY.COM

ABOUT THE AUTHORS

KEN MACGREGOR'S work has appeared in dozens of anthologies and magazines, and the occasional podcast. When not writing, Ken drives the bookmobile for his local library. He lives with his kids, two cats, and the ashes of his wife. Ken can be found at ken-macgregor.com.

KERRY LIPP is the author of several short stories that have been featured in many anthologies and podcasts. A few years ago he fell off the face of the earth, but he comes back to visit every now and then. Headcase is his first novel.